SNOOPY® AND FRIENDS

HERE'S SNOOPY!

Peanuts® characters created
and drawn by Charles M. Schulz

Text by Diane Namm
Background illustrations by Art and Kim Ellis

MERRIGOLD PRESS • NEW YORK

Every morning Charlie Brown brings
Snoopy his breakfast dish.
   "What a great life you have, Snoopy,"
Charlie Brown always says. "Nothing to
worry about, no place to go."

And every morning Snoopy thinks, "That round-headed kid doesn't have a clue about everything I do!"

Do you know what Snoopy does all day?

First he takes his morning run.

Next he does his morning dance.

Then, after all that exercise, Snoopy takes a rest.

At the same time every morning
Snoopy has a snack.

Then it's time for golf.

Snoopy aims his golf club. Then he swings a mighty swing.

But for some reason Snoopy's ball
never goes anywhere!

After golf, it's bowling. Snoopy bowls
with the Beagle Bowling Team.

Uh-oh! The bowling ball is going the
wrong way! Watch out.

Next Snoopy is ready for his tennis lesson. Whoosh! What a serve.

Then Snoopy hurries home for lunch.

After lunch, it's time for Beagle Scouts.

Snoopy leads the scouts into the deep dark woods…

and then the scouts lead Snoopy out!

After scouts, Snoopy paints a picture.

Finally Snoopy becomes the Flying Ace.

He takes his friends for a ride.

By the end of the day Snoopy needs another rest.

When Charlie Brown arrives with
dinner, he can't believe his eyes!
"Snoopy, you haven't moved since I
brought your breakfast dish!"

And Snoopy thinks, "What that round-headed kid doesn't know about me could fill a book!"